The Music Machine

Story by Joy Cowley

One day, a radio
was left in the jungle.

The lion
and the giraffe
and the elephant
wanted the radio.

The lion said,
"I should have
this music machine
because I am fierce.
No one is fiercer
than a lion.
I am the fiercest animal
in the jungle."

The giraffe said,
"No! I should have
the music machine
because I am tall.
No one is taller
than a giraffe.
I am the tallest animal
in the jungle."

The elephant said,
"I am big.
No one is bigger
than an elephant.
I am the biggest animal
in the jungle.
The music machine
should be mine."

Along came the monkey.
"I would like
the music machine,"
the monkey said.

The other animals laughed.

"You are not fierce,"
said the lion.
"You are not tall,"
said the giraffe.
"You are not big,"
said the elephant.

"No," said the monkey.
"I am not any
of those things."

Then the monkey said,
"Listen! What is that noise?"

"What noise?"
said the other animals.

''Hunters! Hunters!''
yelled the monkey.
''Run for your lives!
Hunters are coming
with guns!''

The lion roared,
the giraffe bellowed,
the elephant trumpeted,
and they all ran away
into the jungle.

The monkey climbed a tree.

"I am tricky,"
said the monkey.
"No one is trickier than I am
I am the trickiest animal
in the jungle.
The music machine is mine."